STAR WARS

ADVENTURES IN HYPERSPACE

FIRE R... TO RACE

by Ryd...

D1005028

SCHOLASTIC INC.

New York   Toronto   London   Auckland
Sydney   Mexico City   New Delhi   Hong Kong

www.starwars.com
www.scholastic.com

ISBN 978-0-545-21358-5

12 11 10 9 8 7 6 5 4 3 2 1   10 11 12 13 14 15/0

Cover and interior illustrations by Robert Rath
Printed in the U.S.A.   40
First printing, May 2010

J abba the Hutt dipped his thick, stubby fingers into a barrel filled with two-headed worms. He grabbed one of the fat, squirming creatures and popped it into his wide mouth. He swallowed it with a single gulp. Then he reached back into the barrel and grabbed two more worms. He gobbled up both.

Han Solo said, "All right, Jabba, you've had your taste." Turning to his tall, furry friend, Chewbacca the Wookiee, Han whispered, "I think he likes them."

Han and Chewbacca were standing in Docking Bay 94 at Mos Eisley Spaceport on the sand planet Tatooine. Han's ship, the *Millennium Falcon*, rested on the docking bay's hard floor. They faced Jabba, who had arrived with his Twi'lek assistant Bib Fortuna—and three bodyguards.

Jabba licked his lips as he patted his broad, thick belly. Then he let out a long, rumbling belch.

Glancing at Chewbacca, Han whispered, "I think he likes them a lot."

Bib Fortuna aimed his orange eyes at Han. "Where did you say you obtained these dyad-worms?"

Han grinned. "I *didn't* say, Bib. Does Jabba want to buy the barrel or not?"

Bib Fortuna glanced at the squirming worms, then returned his gaze to Han. "What is your price?"

Han said, "One hundred credits."

Jabba snorted. Fortuna replied nervously, "One hundred is too much!"

Han shrugged. "Oh, well," he said. "There are other buyers."

Jabba chuckled at this. Chewbacca ignored the laughter and kept his eyes on the Hutt's body-guards. If the bodyguards made any sudden moves, Chewbacca was prepared to fire his bow-caster at them.

When Jabba finished laughing, he said, "You amuse me, Solo! I will pay you seventy credits for the worms and another ten if you tell me where you got them."

"Eighty credits for such rare and tasty imports?" Han shook his head. "That hardly  seems fair, Jabba. As for where I got them, I can only say it was far from here. But because you're such a good customer, the barrel is yours for ninety-five credits."

Jabba blinked his heavy eyelids, then said, "Ninety."

Han smiled. "All right, Jabba. You just bought yourself a lot of worms."

Bib paid Han the credits. Chewbacca watched the bodyguards load the barrel onto a repulsor sled. Jabba said, "Solo, how would you like to earn some more money?"

"I'm *always* interested in money, Jabba," Han said. "What's the job?"

"Go to Fornax Station," Jabba said. "Pick up a small cargo container and bring it here."

Han scratched his chin and asked, "Is the container heavy?"

"Not very," Jabba said. "It contains Lashaa silk."

"Lashaa silk, huh?" Han said. "I'm guessing you don't want the station agents to know that you're importing expensive fabric?"

Jabba rolled his eyes. "If I wanted *them* to know, why would I hire *you?*"

"That's true," Han said. "But Fornax Station is a long haul from here. I don't know if I can—"

"I'll pay you two thousand in advance," Jabba interrupted, "and another two thousand on delivery. But if you dare haggle with me again today, I'll hire another pilot."

Han looked at Chewbacca, who had been listening to the conversation. Chewbacca gave a slight nod.

"All right, Jabba," Han said. "We'll get the Lashaa silk for you."

"I know you will, Han," Jabba said. "Because if you don't, I'll be very disappointed." The Hutt nodded to Bib Fortuna and said, "Give Han two thousand credits and the data for the cargo."

Bib paid Han, and then handed him a datacard. Bib said, "This datacard contains the location and passcode for a storage locker where you'll find the Lashaa silk."

Jabba said, "Come along, Fortuna. Our business here is done."

After Jabba and his men left the docking bay, Chewbacca uttered a low growl.

Han replied, "How should I know why Jabba wants Lashaa silk? He doesn't even wear clothes!"

nside the *Millennium Falcon*, Han entered the cockpit. Chewbacca was already seated behind the controls. Han eased into his own seat and said, "The navicomputer is programmed for Fornax Station. Let's go!"

Chewbacca fired the *Falcon*'s jets and guided the ship up through Docking Bay 94's open roof. As the *Falcon* ascended from Mos Eisley, Han said, "Think we should get more worms for Jabba?"

The Wookiee glanced at Han, then responded with a laughing bark.

Han grinned. "I knew Jabba would go for those critters," he said. "Let's hope he never finds out we got them for free. Or that they came from a fertilizer hauler."

Chewbacca tilted back his furry head and roared with glee.

The *Falcon* left Tatooine's atmosphere and entered space, angling away from the sand planet's twin suns. Soon, the ship was beyond Tatooine's gravity field. "All right," Han said. "We're set to jump to hyperspace."

Through the cockpit viewport, Han and Chewbacca saw a field of distant stars. Han pressed a switch. The *Falcon's* hyperdrive engine thundered, and then the stars outside the cockpit appeared to streak over and past the ship.

"I love traveling faster than the speed of light," Han said. "Next stop, Fornax Station."

Chewbacca looked at a datascreen to study their course through hyperspace. He snarled a question.

"Yes, we're going the fastest route," Han replied. "We're taking the Corellian Run to the Hydian Way. Then we slide onto the Braxant Run, and then to—"

Chewbacca interrupted with a series of sharp grunts.

"Forget the Namadii Corridor!" Han answered. "Remember the traffic?!"

Chewbacca shook his head. He pointed at the navigational console and grunted again.

Han replied, "Oh, yeah? Well, we'll take the Namadii Corridor on the way back to Tatooine. If your way is faster than mine, I'll buy you a bantha rump."

Bantha rump was one of Chewbacca's favorite meals. He replied with a cheerful howl.

Han and Chewbacca were an unusual pair. Han was from Corellia, and had once trained to be an Imperial pilot. Chewbacca the Wookiee was over 200 years old, and came from the jungle planet Kashyyyk. They liked working together, and hated the Empire. They had been friends for years.

"The autopilot is working fine," Han said. "C'mon, pal. Let's run a systems check on the engines. After that, we can pass the time with a game of dejarik."

Chewbacca liked playing the holomonster game. He followed Han out of the cockpit and went to the engineering station in the main hold. When they finished checking the engines, they sat down beside their circular game table.

Chewbacca barked a question.

"Sure, Chewie," Han said. "We'll play 'til I lose. But no cheating!"

Several hours later, Han and Chewbacca were still hunkered over the game table when an audio signal chirped from the engineering station. "You heard the signal, Chewie," Han said as he jumped up from his seat. "We're about to exit hyperspace."

Chewbacca remained at the table and roared in protest.

Han replied, "Haven't you won enough games already?"

The Wookiee roared again. He swatted the game board so hard that he made the holomonsters jump.

"If you break the table," Han said sternly, "I'm not buying a new one."

Chewbacca wouldn't budge.

Han thought for a moment, then said, "Oh, well. Guess you'll miss the Fire Rings."

Chewbacca murmured curiously.

"What?" Han gasped. "You've never seen the Five Fire Rings of Fornax?"

The Wookiee shook his head.

"Well, they're only one of the greatest natural wonders of the galaxy. But . . . hey, you don't have to take my word for it, pal. If you'd rather sit here and watch holomonsters clobber each other—"

Chewbacca jumped up from the game table and brushed past Han, nearly knocking him over. As the Wookiee scrambled toward the cockpit, Han rolled his eyes and muttered, "I hope he's not disappointed."

Han arrived beside Chewbacca in the cockpit just as the *Millennium Falcon* dropped out of
hyperspace. They found themselves looking out
upon the planet Fornax and an orbital space station. Fornax was a bright world, and appeared to
be encircled by five
rings of fire.

Han said,
"Impressed?"

Chewbacca
nodded and
murmured his
approval.

"Good," Han said as he steered the *Falcon*
toward Fornax Station. "Now let's get Jabba's
stuff."

* * *

But as the *Falcon* drew closer to Fornax Station, an alarm sounded in the cockpit.

Han glanced at a sensor scope. "Looks like we have some unexpected company, Chewie. Our scanner is picking up an Imperial ship's signal!"

Many ships were visible outside Fornax Station. Chewbacca looked at them and growled menacingly.

"No," Han replied. "The signal's coming from somewhere *inside* the station." A moment later, he added, "I hate surprises!"

Han and Chewbacca saw their cockpit's comm unit blink on. From the comm, a woman's voice spoke.

"Fornax Station Flight Control to approaching Corellian YT-1300 freighter *Close Shave*," the controller said. "Do you copy, *Close Shave*?"

"Loud and clear," Han answered. He winked at Chewbacca. They had adjusted their ship's transponder to identify the *Falcon* as the *Close Shave*, a fake name. "My copilot and I are just passing through," Han continued. "Thought we'd see the Fire Rings. May we have permission to dock?"

The controller directed Han toward Docking Bay 21, where an invisible tractor beam locked onto the *Millennium Falcon*. Han and Chewbacca remained seated in the cockpit while the station's tractor beam pulled their ship into the docking bay.

"Good thing we rigged the *Falcon*'s transponder with a fake name," Han said. "You never know who you might run into on a space station. If there are any Imperial ships in the area, we don't want them to notice us."

Chewbacca growled a question.

"Don't ask *me* why the Empire has any interest in Fornax," Han replied. "All I know is that when the *Falcon* picks up an Imperial signal, we don't turn and run. That would only attract attention. The best thing is to remain calm. We'll go about our business like everything's normal."

Chewbacca growled another question.

"Well, if *that* happens," Han answered, "we fire our weapons at everything in sight, and *then* we turn and run."

Chewbacca whimpered nervously.

"Don't worry, Chewie," Han said. "We're just picking up a small cargo container. What could possibly go wrong?"

After the tractor beam placed the *Falcon* inside the docking bay, Han and Chewbacca secured their ship and headed into the station. Chewbacca brought a bulky travel bag with him. From what they could see, Fornax was a popular destination for tourists from all over the galaxy.

As they made their way through the crowd, Chewbacca overheard a tour guide explain, "The rings are actually solar prominences. Fornax attracts them from its own sun."

Han noticed Chewbacca trying to glimpse the
Fire Rings through a window. "Stop gawking, fuzz-
ball," Han whispered. "And keep your eyes peeled
for Imperials!"

Han was still trying to guide Chewbacca away from the windows when he accidentally bumped into a tall man who wore an expensive cape. Spinning fast, the caped man bellowed, "Watch where you're going!"

Chewbacca moved in front of Han and snarled fiercely. The startled man stumbled backward.

"Relax, Chewie," Han said. "We don't want trouble." He faced the man and added, "My fault. Sorry."

It was only then that Han noticed a group of about twenty other well-dressed people viewing Fornax through a nearby window. A young woman in an elegant gown turned from the window, saw Han and Chewbacca, and moved toward them. She stopped beside the caped man and said, "What's going on here?"

Han said, "I was just apologizing to—"

Silencing Han with a glare, the woman snapped, "I am the Royal Margravine Abominelle of Vena! How dare you spoil my holiday!"

"I don't dare nothin', Your Abominableness," Han said as he breezed past her. "You're spoiled enough already."

The woman's mouth fell open. She was stunned speechless.

Leaving the fuming woman behind, Han and Chewbacca spotted an information center. An illuminated sign gave directions to the space station's storage center.

Han reached into his vest pocket and removed the datacard that Bib Fortuna had given him. "According to this datacard," Han said, "Jabba's cargo container is in locker B-392."

Chewbacca was about to turn away from the information center when Han grabbed the Wookiee's arm and said, "Hang on. I think I just found someone who might be able to tell us if any Imperial soldiers are on board."

Chewbacca followed Han's gaze to see an ancient, four-armed droid standing beside a shoeshine stand. The stand had two seats. Both were unoccupied.

Han stepped over to the stand and climbed up into one of the seats. He glanced down at the old droid and said, "How about a shine, pal?"

"Really?" rasped the droid. He swiveled his photoreceptors to look at Han's black boots. Then the droid looked back up at the seated man's face. "You really want me to polish your boots?"

"That's what you *do*, isn't it?" Han asked.

"Yes, boots are my specialty!" the droid said brightly. "But I'm afraid I don't work as much as I'd like." As he began rubbing polish onto Han's boots, he continued, "Few people care about how their boots look anymore . . . or appreciate decent footwear." The droid glanced at the nearby Wookiee's fur-covered feet.

Chewbacca snarled.

"I mean no offense," the droid said.

Han said casually, "If you want more work, maybe you should move to Imperial space."

"Oh?" the droid said as his lower arms buffed Han's boots. "Why there?"

Han shrugged. "You got me thinking about who has lots of boots to clean. The first thing I thought of was stormtroopers."

The droid said, "I've heard that stormtroopers can be most unkind to droids. I think I'd prefer to remain here."

Han said, "I guess stormtroopers would be a rare sight on Fornax Station."

"I've never seen one," the droid replied.

"Well, thanks for the shine," Han said. He rose from the seat.

Swiping at Han's left boot, the droid said, "I'm not done!"

"But I am," said Han with a grin.

Han and Chewbacca stepped away from the shoeshine station. Han muttered, "Pretty clever, huh?"

Chewbacca murmured in response.

Han replied, "No, I can't explain the Imperial signal we intercepted. But let's just finish the job here."

As they walked off, they didn't notice the shoeshine droid raise one arm and speak into a transmitter. "A man seemed curious about stormtroopers," the droid whispered. "He's heading for the storage center."

A droid clerk stood at the entrance of Fornax Station's storage center. The droid held a comlink up beside her audio sensor, listening. As Han and Chewbacca approached the entrance, the droid returned the comlink to a slot in her metal skirt. The droid turned to face them and asked, "May I help you?"

Han pointed to Chewbacca's travel bag and said, "My friend would like a locker to stow his luggage."

The droid nodded and said, "Right this way, please."

The droid led Han and Chewbacca to an aisle that was lined with numbered lockers. All the locker doors were secured by keypad locks. As they moved past the lockers, Han searched the numbers until he found B-392.

The droid gestured to a different locker on the opposite wall. She said, "I think you'll find this locker is large enough." She tapped the locker's keypad and its door slid open.

"Thanks," Han said. "You can go now."

"Sorry," the droid said. "I'm required to observe all customer transactions. There have been reports of smugglers using the lockers to hide merchandise."

"Smugglers?" Han said. "Gee, that's terrible. Isn't it, Chewie?"

Chewbacca groaned.

Suddenly, a buzzer sounded from the far end of the aisle. Hearing the buzzer, the droid clerk said, "Oh, dear. Another customer."

Facing the droid, Han said, "It'll take my friend a minute to check some things in his luggage before we stow it in the locker. If you go see the other customer, we'll meet you out front."

"Well . . . all right," the droid said. She turned and wheeled quickly out of the aisle. As soon as she was gone, Han and Chewbacca stepped over to locker B-392. They stared cautiously at the keypad.

Han whispered, "Do you remember seeing a buzzer at the entrance?"

Chewbacca snarled.

"I didn't see a buzzer, either," Han replied. "And that droid seemed eager to leave us here. "

He motioned Chewbacca back to the locker that the droid had opened for them. They peered into the locker. It was empty. Han said, "Think this is some kind of trap?"

Chewbacca snarled again.

"Only one way to find out," Han said. He took Chewbacca's travel bag, shoved it inside the locker, and shut the door.

And then the alarm went off.

The alarm whooped loudly. Chewbacca and Han flung their hands up over their ears.

A moment later, the alarm stopped. While their ears were still ringing, they heard a man's voice from behind. "Keep your hands away from your weapons! And turn around slowly!"

Han and Chewbacca followed the man's instructions. They turned to face a security officer in a rumpled uniform with two droids.

Han said, "What's going on here?"

"I'm Chief Smurdap, head of Fornax Security," the man declared. "And you're suspected of smuggling."

"Smuggling?!" Han said, looking astonished. "Us?"

Chief Smurdap said, "I know you were seeking information about Imperial activity on Fornax Station . . . perhaps because you're a fugitive from the Empire?"

"Huh?" Han said. He shook his head. "Oh . . . maybe you overheard me talking to a shoeshine droid earlier. The droid said something like, 'I wish I shined more boots,' and I said, 'Maybe you should try working in Imperial space, because there's lots of stormtroopers who need their boots polished,' and he said—"

"Enough!" Chief Smurdap interrupted. "I demand to see what you put in that locker!"

Han grinned at the security chief. He said, "Take it easy. We've got nothing to hide." Keeping his hands held high, he let his eyes flick to the locker that held Chewbacca's travel bag. "Go on," he said. "Help yourself."

Chief Smurdap gave a slight nod to one of the two security droids. The droid extended a metal finger to tap at the locker door's keypad. The locker door slid open. The droid yanked out Chewbacca's knapsack.

Smurdap watched as the droid pried open the bag to reveal combs, brushes, and bottles of scented liquid. Smurdap said, "Grooming supplies?!"

Han said, "Sure, didn't you know? Our ship is the *Close Shave*. We're freelance barbers."

Smurdap removed a large comb from the bag and examined it. Han said, "Careful with that one. It's a hand-carved Wookiee special!"

Smurdap's face went red with rage. "It appears there has been a misunderstanding," he said as he dropped the comb back into the bag. "You are free to go about your business." He turned and left. The security droids followed him.

The instant the security chief and droids were
out of sight, Han turned to Chewbacca and said,
"See, I told you those old brushes and combs
might come in handy! Now, let's do the switch."

Moving fast, Han used Jabba's datacard to
open locker B-392. Inside was a small cargo con-

tainer. While Han pulled the container out of the
locker, Chewbacca quickly removed the grooming
supplies from the bag and dumped them into the
other open locker. They shut both locker doors,
then stuffed the cargo container into the bag.

Chewbacca picked up the bag that now concealed the cargo container. He followed Han back to the storage center's entrance.

The droid clerk saw the approaching man and Wookiee. Looking at the bag, she said nervously, "You . . . don't want the locker?"

"What do you think?!" Han snapped. "It's not *our* fault if you have a smuggling problem! We've never been so insulted! We're leaving!"

Han and Chewbacca kept walking. They didn't look back.

After leaving Fornax Station's storage center, Han and Chewbacca walked back to the shoeshine stand they had visited earlier. When the shoeshine droid saw them, his photoreceptors jerked back with surprise.

"Oh!" the little droid exclaimed. "Everything all right? Did you, uh, want another shine?"

"No," Han said flatly. "You've done enough already."

Chewbacca bent forward and growled at the droid. The droid trembled nervously and said, "Please don't tear me apart!"

Facing the droid, Han said, "*You* sent Fornax Security after us."

"Nothing personal!" the droid cried. "Chief Smurdap ordered all droids to report anyone who asked suspicious questions!"

Chewbacca growled again. The droid trembled so hard that his parts clattered.

"Take it easy, Chewie," Han said. Returning his attention to the droid, he said calmly, "If you

search your memory banks, you'll recall that all *I* asked for was a shoeshine. But don't worry. I told Chief Smurdap it was just a misunderstanding."

"Oh," said the droid. "I . . . I'm sorry for any inconvenience."

"I realize you're only doing your job," Han said, "just like Chief Smurdap. He certainly takes his work seriously."

The droid nodded and said, "Chief Smurdap is a former Imperial Customs agent. He's *very* determined to capture thieves and smugglers!"

"Imperial Customs, huh?" Han said. "Well, he sure is a long way from Imperial space in this—"

Suddenly, a woman's scream echoed down the corridor. Chewbacca reacted immediately, bolting off in the direction of the scream. Han hollered, "Wait for me!"

Leaving the shoeshine stand, Han chased Chewbacca around a corner. The Wookiee came to a sudden halt, and Han nearly ran into him. They had both stopped short of the screaming woman, who stood beside a hovering luggage sled, along with the caped man whom Han had bumped into earlier.

They recognized Margravine Abominelle immediately.

Seeing Han, the woman screamed again.

Han said, "What's wrong?!"

"My wedding gown!" she shrieked as she pointed to the luggage sled. "It's been stolen!"

"Wedding gown?" Han said with annoyance. "Suffering comets, lady! Ya shouldn't scream like that unless it's an emergency!"

The woman glared at Han. "Again, you insult the Royal Margravine Abominelle," she said scornfully. "And on the eve of my wedding day! If we were on Vena, I should have you imprisoned."

"But we're not on Vena," Han said, "so why don't you go jump through a Fire Ring!"

The woman gasped as her eyes went wide.

Pointing to her open mouth, Han said, "You should get that fixed."

Leaving the stunned woman, Han walked off with Chewbacca at his side. Han said, "If what that shoeshine droid said is true about Chief Smurdap being a former Imperial, that might explain why we picked up an Imperial signal earlier. Smurdap could be using a decommissioned Imperial ship or surplus transmitter."

Chewbacca groaned.

Han replied, "Why didn't you say so sooner? Sure, we can get a closer view of the Fire Rings before we go back to Tatooine!"

They returned to the docking bay that held the *Falcon*. Inside their ship, they removed

Jabba's cargo container from the travel bag and stowed it in a hidden compartment beneath the floor. Then they went to the cockpit.

Han contacted Fornax Flight Control. "This is the captain of the *Close Shave*," he said. "May we have clearance for departure?"

The station's flight controller replied, "That's a negative, *Close Shave*."

Keeping his voice calm, Han asked, "May I ask *why* we can't leave?"

"Orders from Fornax Security," the flight controller answered from the *Falcon*'s comm. "No arrivals or departures until further notice."

Han switched off the comm. He said, "I'm getting very tempted to blast our way out of here."

Just then, from the cockpit, Han and Chewbacca saw Chief Smurdap and two security droids enter the docking bay. Smurdap didn't look happy.

Exit your ship at once!" Chief Smurdap called out from the docking bay floor. "And leave your weapons inside!"

Inside the *Falcon*'s cockpit, Han glanced at Chewbacca. Han said, "If we ever want to return to Fornax Station, we should play nice. But if Smurdap's droids try anything funny, we'll introduce them to our 'Ground Buzzer.'" Han flicked a switch to set the *Falcon*'s concealed blaster cannon on automatic.

Chewbacca made a chuckling noise as he followed Han out of the cockpit.

Han removed his blaster pistol from the holster at his side and left it in the main hold. They lowered the *Falcon*'s landing ramp and walked down it. They faced Smurdap and his droids. One of the droids was carrying a plastoid box.

Smurdap pointed at the *Falcon* and said smugly, "I suppose this is your flying barber shop?"

Han shrugged. "The *Close Shave* gets us where we have to go," he said.

Smurdap grinned. He said, "I found something interesting in your locker at the storage center." He gestured to the droid who carried the box. The droid tilted the box, and dumped the abandoned grooming supplies onto the floor.

Han rolled his eyes, then stared hard at Chewbacca and said under his breath, "I *told* you we should have just thrown that stuff out! But no, you *had* to leave it all in the locker!"

Chewbacca lowered his head and whimpered.

Impatient, Smurdap said, "Why did you leave these things?!"

Han replied, "Well, don't take this the wrong way, Chief, but . . . some Wookiees think if other people touch their stuff, their stuff gets spoiled."

Chewbacca whimpered again.

"Because you held his best comb earlier," Han continued, "he thinks you spoiled *all* his supplies. I told him to chuck it all, but he left everything in the locker because he thought someone else might find a good use for them."

Smurdap snickered. "That's quite a story," he said. "But there's just one problem with it. The storage center's droid clerk told me that you left carrying a *full* bag!"

Han shook his head. "The clerk's mistaken," he said.

"Really?" said Smurdap. He smiled, displaying several crooked teeth. "There has been a theft on Fornax Station. That's why I ordered Flight Control to stop all ships from leaving. Would you know anything about a missing wedding gown?"

Han raised his eyebrows. "Wedding gown?" He glanced at Chewbacca and decided to tell the truth. "Now that you mention it, we did hear a dame yammering that someone had stolen hers."

"It's worth a fortune," Chief Smurdap said. "It's made of Tyrian shimmersilk."

Because they were transporting Lashaa silk for Jabba, both Han and Chewbacca were surprised to hear the word *silk*, but they didn't show it. "Oh," Han said. "I guess that explains why the bride-to-be was so upset."

Smurdap smiled at Han and Chewbacca. It wasn't a pleasant smile. He said, "You'll remain here while I inspect your ship. If you move, you'll be shot."

Smurdap gestured to one security droid, which promptly aimed its blaster rifle at Han and Chewbacca. The other droid followed Smurdap up the *Falcon*'s landing ramp and into the ship.

Keeping his eyes on the droid that guarded them, Chewbacca grunted a question to Han.

"Don't worry about Jabba's container," Han whispered back. "*His* silk is safe! I can't say we have nothing to hide, Chewie, but I *can* say that Smurdap won't find it."

Less than three minutes later, Smurdap and the droid stepped out of the *Falcon*. The droid was carrying Chewbacca's travel bag. Han noticed the travel bag appeared to be no longer empty. He also noticed the security officer's own boots had not been polished recently.

The droid held out the bag and Smurdap reached into it. He pulled out a luxurious shimmer-silk gown.

Chewbacca snarled. Han replied, "It's not my size, either."

While the droids kept their weapons aimed at Han and Chewbacca, Chief Smurdap leered. "It appears the clerk droid was correct," Smurdap said. "Your bag *was* full when you left the storage center. I expect the margravine from Vena will be most grateful for the return of her wedding gown."

Han grinned. "She'll probably give you a big reward, Smurdap. That is, unless she finds out that it was you who stole her gown and then faked finding it on my ship."

Chief Smurdap stuffed the expensive gown back into the bag. Facing Han, he said, "I doubt very much the margravine will ever hear an accusation against me."

"Let me guess," Han said. "After you stole the gown, you hid it in a compartment inside the droid that boarded my ship with you. Then you placed the gown in my friend's travel bag."

Smurdap said, "And why would I do that?"

"Because you needed someone to blame for the theft," Han continued. "Also, you figured if my friend and I *did* leave the storage center with a full bag, we might have taken something valuable. . . . Maybe something we could give to you in exchange for letting us go."

Smurdap smiled. "You're close, but not quite," he said. "I'm *certain* you two took something valuable. I intend to have it. And I don't plan on letting you leave Fornax Station. At least not alive."

Han sighed. "Well, I guess there's no more point in playing nice," he said. He looked at Chewbacca and shouted loudly, "Fire!"

In response to Han's command, something popped out of the *Falcon*'s lower hull. It was the ship's automatic blaster cannon. As Han and Chewie leaped away from Smurdap and the droids, the Ground Buzzer opened fire.

The security droids didn't react fast enough to the *Falcon*'s cannon. The first volley of blaster bolts cut one droid in half. The other droid managed to squeeze off a single shot at the ceiling but was downed by another hail of blaster fire. Smurdap shouted as he ran for the docking bay's exit.

Scrambling up the *Falcon*'s landing ramp, Han
shouted "Chewie! Grab the travel bag!"

Hot on Han's heels, Chewbacca seized the bag
and the dress, and sprinted into the *Falcon*.

The docking bay's emergency alarms began blaring, and the Ground Buzzer was still firing as Han raised the *Falcon*'s ramp and sealed the hatch. Chewbacca tossed the travel bag into the main hold.

As Han chased Chewbacca to the cockpit, he noticed the floor panels were still in place over the hidden compartment. *Jabba's cargo is safe!* They entered the cockpit and jumped behind the controls. "Start the engines!" Han said. "Fast!"

Chewbacca threw switches and pressed buttons. He wailed a question.

"Let *me* deal with Flight Control!" Han replied as he switched off the Ground Buzzer. "Just be ready to launch!"

Two quad laser cannon turrets were located at the top and bottom of the *Falcon*. The quad laser cannons were more powerful than the Ground

Buzzer. Although the laser cannons were more accurate when fired from the turrets, Han had rigged them to a control stick inside the cockpit.

Han was not very concerned about accuracy at the moment. He activated the upper laser cannon, aimed in the general direction of the docking bay's tractor-beam projector, and squeezed the trigger.

An instant later, Han's target exploded.

More alarms sounded in the docking bay. Robotic ceiling-mounted fire extinguishers sprayed at the blazing wreckage. Han aimed the cannons at a fuel storage tank and fired again. The explosion was incredible.

As the docking bay rapidly filled with fire and smoke, Han activated the comm unit. "Flight Control!" he shouted. "We have a weapons malfunction in Docking Bay 21! Request emergency evacuation!"

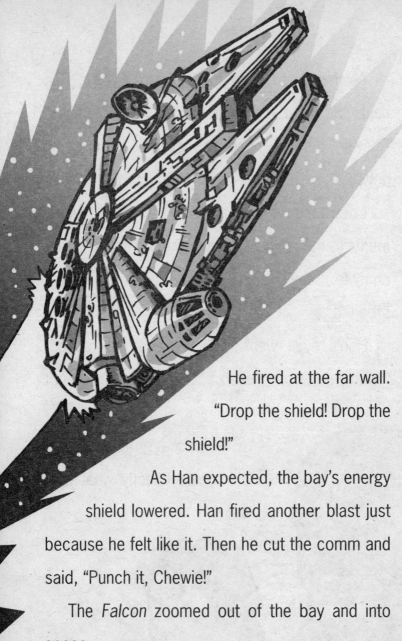

He fired at the far wall.

"Drop the shield! Drop the shield!"

As Han expected, the bay's energy shield lowered. Han fired another blast just because he felt like it. Then he cut the comm and said, "Punch it, Chewie!"

The *Falcon* zoomed out of the bay and into space.

As they sped away from Fornax Station, Han said, "Sorry to ruin your tour of the Fire Rings, Chewie, but we need to get into hyperspace now!"

Chewbacca made a quick series of adjustments to the controls. A red light flashed on a data console. Chewie pointed to the flashing light and groaned.

Han's eyes went wide. "What?!" he replied, "What do you *mean*, the hyperdrive's not working?!"

Chewbacca groaned again. He'd meant exactly what he'd said.

Han shook his head. "Why would the hyperdrive malfunction *now*?!" But as soon as the words were out of his mouth, he thought, *Smurdap*!

Chewbacca let out a woeful yowl.

Han said, "Maintain this course, Chewie. Put as much distance between us and Fornax Station as you can. I need to check something."

Han bolted from the cockpit. He entered the main hold, nearly stumbled over Chewie's travel bag, and quickly inspected the engineering station. What he found made him feel ill.

Han switched on the engineering station's comlink and said, "Chewie, can you hear me?"

Chewbacca's responsive grunts sounded from the comlink's speaker.

"Good news and bad news," Han replied. "First, the bad news. When Smurdap and his droid boarded our ship, they didn't just stuff a wedding gown into your bag. They also locked a circuit-jammer onto the engineering console to shut down our hyperdrive."

Hearing this, Chewbacca roared so loud that Han could hear him from the main hold without the comlink.

"Yeah, I'm not thrilled about it, either," Han answered. "But here's the good news. I think I can remove the jammer, but it'll take time to—"

Han was interrupted by an unexpected rumble of explosive bursts from outside the ship. The *Falcon* shuddered violently. "Chewie!" Han shouted, "Who's shooting at us?!"

Chewbacca answered with a hoot and a snort.

"An Imperial signal?!" Han replied with surprise. "That must be Smurdap's ship!"

Removing the circuit-jammer would have to wait. Han ran for the access tube that led to the *Falcon*'s laser-cannon turrets.

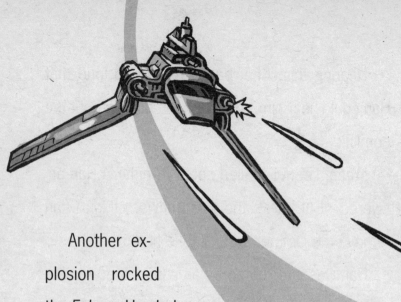

Another explosion rocked the *Falcon*. Han hollered, "Take evasive action, Chewie!"

Han grabbed ahold of the ladder that extended between the upper and lower turrets. He climbed quickly up the ladder and settled into the swivel-mounted gunner's seat. Slapping a comlink around his head, he seized the cannon's trigger-grips and shouted, "Chewie! I'm in the dorsal turret!"

Suddenly, green laserfire streaked past Han's turret and pounded at the *Falcon*'s deflector shields. Han swung the cannons to sight the enemy ship. It was an old Mu-2 long-range shuttle with a pair of fire-linked forward laser cannons.

Han adjusted the cannon's targeting computer and aimed at the incoming shuttle.

Han squeezed the cannon's triggers, launching red laserbolts at the Mu-2 shuttle. The first three bolts sailed past his target, but the fourth made a bright burst as it impacted against the shuttle's deflector shield. Han exclaimed, "Ha!"

The shuttle veered away from the *Falcon*. Han was about to fire again when he heard Chewbacca bark from the comlink. Han replied, "A transmission from Smurdap? Patch it through."

A few seconds passed, and then Han heard Smurdap's voice. "That's quite a ship," Smurdap said. "For 'barbers,' you're very well-armed!"

"If you pull over," Han replied, "the Wookiee and I will be happy to give you a free clip."

"I bet you would," Smurdap said. "Let's stop kidding around. You can't escape the Fornax System, not with a disabled hyperdrive. Give me the shimmersilk gown and your cargo, and I'll unlock the circuit-jammer."

Han laughed. "I don't bargain with sleemos who sabotage my ship."

"If you don't deal with me," Smurdap said, "you'll have to deal with my reinforcements."

Han thought, *What reinforcements?* And then he saw the approaching starfighters.

Six drone starfighters raced away from Fornax Station, heading straight for the *Falcon*. Chewbacca saw them, too, and wailed over the comm.

Furious, Han fired his cannons at Smurdap's shuttle. As Smurdap took evasive action, Han scrambled out of the turret and raced back to the cockpit.

"Hey, Chewie!" Han said as he practically fell into the pilot's seat. "Ready for that tour of the Fire Rings?"

Chewbacca shook his head and howled.

The six drone starfighters looked nearly identical. Each was a sleek projectile, little more than an unshielded laser cannon with maneuverable wings and a droid brain. All raced across space like deadly darts, heading straight for the *Millennium Falcon*.

Han steered the *Falcon* toward the brightly ringed planet, and then he gunned the sublight engine. "We may not be able to reach lightspeed, Chewie," he said, "but we can still give those drones a good race!"

Chewbacca shook his head again and let out a pleading whimper.

"Sorry, Chewie," Han replied. "I can't say I know any pilot who's flown through the Five Fire Rings of Fornax and survived. But I can't see any other way to shake those drones."

The *Falcon*'s comm was still on, transmitting Han and Chewbacca's conversation to Chief Smurdap's shuttle. Smurdap said, "You're bluffing."

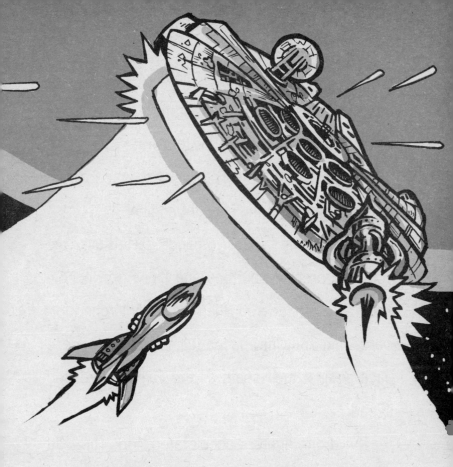

Han laughed. "You want what's on our ship, Smurdap? Come and get it!" Then he flicked off the comm unit and said, "Don't worry, Chewie. I know what I'm doing."

Han glanced at a sensor scope. The drone starfighters were coming in fast.

The lead drone fighter fired at the *Falcon*. Laserfire pounded at the freighter's aft deflector shield. Chewbacca barked with alarm.

Han answered, "Divert power from the forward deflector shield to the sublight engine!"

The Wookiee's massive hands darted over the controls, pressing buttons and flipping switches. The *Falcon* shuddered, then suddenly lurched forward. Han and Chewbacca felt their bodies press back against their seats as the *Falcon* increased speed.

The drone fighters accelerated, too. The lead drone fired again.

"Buckle up tight, Chewie," Han said as he secured his own safety belt. "This is gonna hurt!" He heard Chewbacca's belt snap into place, then threw a switch to make the *Falcon* rapidly decrease speed.

Trailing behind the *Falcon*, the lead drone and a second fighter were still traveling at high velocity. Neither fighter was able to slow down or escape a collision. Both struck and shattered against the freighter's rear deflector shields. The *Falcon* bounced at the impact, but her shields held.

"Ha!" Han shouted as he gunned the sublight engine and zoomed off, still on course for the rings of Fornax.

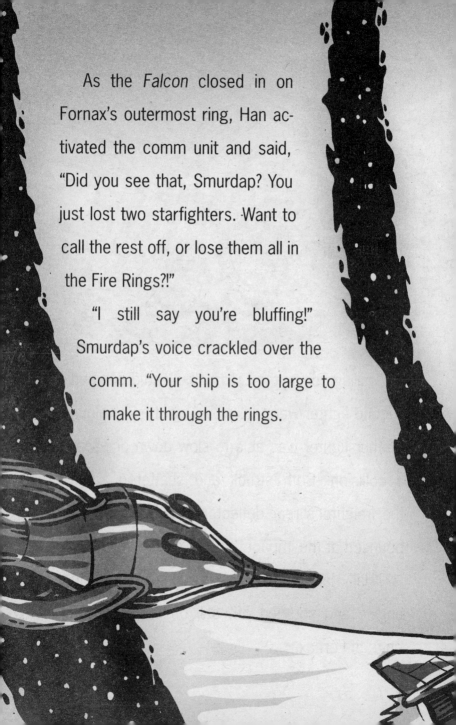

As the *Falcon* closed in on Fornax's outermost ring, Han activated the comm unit and said, "Did you see that, Smurdap? You just lost two starfighters. Want to call the rest off, or lose them all in the Fire Rings?!"

"I still say you're bluffing!" Smurdap's voice crackled over the comm. "Your ship is too large to make it through the rings.

"Have it your way," Han said. He switched off the comm and guided the *Falcon* into a steep dive. "Divert power to forward shields, Chewie! We're goin' in!"

Chewbacca groaned as he followed Han's command. And then the *Falcon* plunged into the brilliant ring.

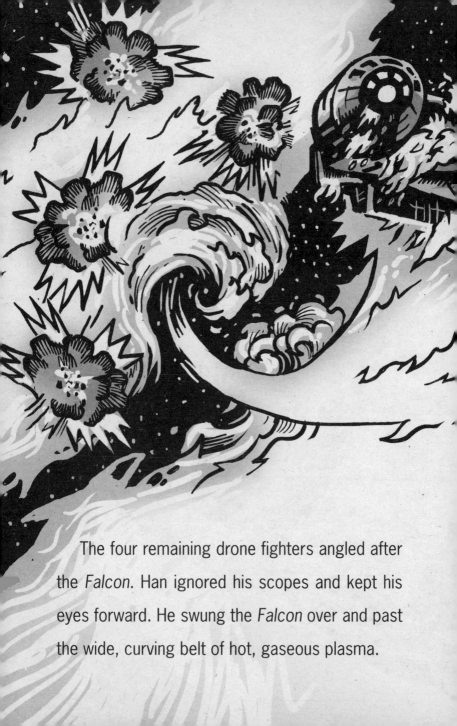

The four remaining drone fighters angled after
the *Falcon*. Han ignored his scopes and kept his
eyes forward. He swung the *Falcon* over and past
the wide, curving belt of hot, gaseous plasma.

Chewbacca yelped as the *Falcon* dipped below
what appeared to be a wall of blazing dust.
In the next instant, four distinct explosions
sounded from outside.

"There go the drones," Han said.
"Without deflector shields, they never stood a chance in this heat!"

Han pulled back on the controls, and the *Falcon* lifted out of the rings. "*Now*, we deal with Smurdap," he said. "But we do it *my* way."

He made an adjustment to the *Falcon*'s radio transceiver, and then switched on the comm. Chewbacca guessed what Han was about to do, and found himself grinning.

"Hey, Smurdap!" Han said into the comm. "Still want the dress that you stole from the margravine of Vena?"

After a brief silence, Smurdap responded from his shuttle, "You *know* I want it!"

"Swell," Han said. "All you have to do is apologize to me and my furry friend for trying to frame us for your dirty work."

"Is that all?" Smurdap answered. "Fine! I'm very, very sorry I tried to blame you and the Wookiee for stealing the shimmersilk gown. Now, how do you propose you hand it over to me?"

Han said, "I suggest we both fly back to Fornax Station. Did you hear all that, Flight Control?"

Much to Smurdap's surprise, the voice of Fornax Station's flight controller replied, "Loud and clear, *Close Shave*. The new security chief will be very eager to listen to Smurdap's confession!"

Over the comm, Smurdap stammered, "You . . . I . . . he . . . he's lying!"

"Tell it to the margravine!" Han replied from the *Falcon.* "And before you get any ideas about making a run for it, you should know that Chewie and I have our cannons trained on your ship!"

Chewbacca roared into the comm.

"Sure, Chewie," Han said. "If Smurdap tries to escape on the way back to Fornax Station, I'll let *you* do the shooting!"

Margravine Abominelle of Vena will see you now," said the margravine's protocol droid.

"Thanks," Han said. "C'mon, Chewie."

Chewbacca followed Han into the margravine's suite on Fornax Station. Inside, they found the margravine holding the gown. She looked at them and said, "Your ship has been repaired?"

"Yup," Han said. "And Chief Smurdap has been arrested. We were just about to leave."

The margravine tossed the gown into a corner and declared, "The wedding is off!"

Han and Chewbacca looked at the priceless dress on the floor, then lifted their eyes to the margravine. Han said, "That's too bad. Chewie and I went to a lot of trouble to get your gown back."

The margravine smiled and fixed Han with her gaze. "Do you know *why* I called off the wedding?" Before Han could answer, she announced, "I have fallen in love . . . with someone *else*!"

"Oh," Han said. "That's nice. I mean, too bad for the other guy, but—"

"He is like no one else I have ever met," the margravine interrupted. Her arm darted out and she seized Han's hand in her own.

Han looked at the margravine's hand and politely shook it. "I'm sure he's a very special fellow. But see, Chewie here, *he* was wondering if maybe there, uh, might be a reward for the gown?"

The margravine's eyes went wide. She yanked her hand back. And then her face flushed with rage and she began to scream.

Han winced and put his hands over his ears. Chewbacca grabbed his friend and hauled him out of the suite.

"What was *with* that lady?" Han said after they returned to the *Millennium Falcon*. "All I did was mention a reward! I tell ya, I'm *sorry* for the guy she fell in love with!"

Chewbacca rolled his eyes.

"Say 'so long' to Fornax Station," Han said. "All set for the jump back to Tatooine?"

Chewbacca nodded, and then barked a question.

"Sure, the hyperdrive's working!" Han said. "Watch this!"

An instant later, the *Falcon* vanished into hyperspace.

BE A PART OF *THE CLONE WARS*™ ACTION!

*"I don't fight for Jedi or Sith. I work for the **highest bidder**."*

STAR WARS
THE CLONE WARS™

The war between the heroic Jedi and the evil Sith continues, and ruthless bounty hunter Cad Bane's in the middle of it all! Collect him and *all* the other 3¾" figures, and battle on!

Cad Bane™

Anakin Skywalker™

Hondo Ohnaka™

Clone Commander Stone™

Clone Trooper Jek™

Captain Rex™